Super STEM Activities

Amazing Activities with

SOUND and HEARING

Anne O'Daly

Published in 2023 by Enslow Publishing, LLC
29 East 21st Street, New York, NY 10010

Design Manager: Keith Davis
Design and Illustration: squareandcircus.co.uk

Manufactured in the United States of America

CPSIA compliance information: Batch #CSENS23: For further information contact Enslow Publishing LLC, New York, New York at 1-800-398-2504.

Please visit our website, www.enslowpublishing.com. For a free color catalog of all our high-quality books, call toll free 1-800-398-2504 or fax 1-877-980-4454.

Cataloging-in-Publication Data

Names: O'Daly, Anne.
Title: Amazing activities with sound and hearing / Anne O'Daly.
Description: New York : Enslow Publishing, 2023. | Series: Super STEM Activities | Includes glossary and index.
Identifiers: ISBN 9781978529663 (pbk.) | ISBN 9781978529687 (library bound) | ISBN 9781978529670 (6pack) | ISBN 9781978529694 (ebook)
Subjects: LCSH: Sound--Experiments--Juvenile literature.
Classification: LCC QC225.5 O339 2023 | DDC 534.078--dc23

CONTENTS

What is sound? 4
Think like a scientist! 6
Bouncing waves 8
Spot the noise 10
Speed of sound 12
Tuning fork 14
Balloon sound 16
Pluck a string 18
Pan pipes 20
Make a beat 22
Block the noise 24
Build a bull-roarer 26
A clap of thunder 28
Glossary 30
Further resources 31
Index 32

WHAT IS SOUND?

Sound is all around us. It can be quiet or loud. It can be pleasant or not. We use sound to communicate and we make different sounds on instruments to make music. But what is sound, and how is it made?

Sound is made when something vibrates (moves back and forth very quickly). If you bang a drum, you can hear the sound the vibrations make. You can see the drum's skin vibrate. If an object vibrates, the vibrations travel through the air. When they reach your ears, you hear them as sound.

Sound waves

Sound is a kind of energy. It moves in invisible patterns called sound waves. When an object vibrates in the air, it pushes on the particles next to the surface of the object. These particles push on the ones next to them, and so on, to make a wave.

The type of sound depends on the size and speed of the sound. Loud sounds are made by big vibrations. Big vibrations make tall sound waves. A drum makes a louder noise when it is hit firmly. Quiet sounds have smaller vibrations and smaller sound waves.

WAVELENGTH AND FREQUENCY

Sound waves have high points (crests) and low points (troughs), with regular spaces in between. The distance between the troughs is called the wavelength. If a sound wave has a long wavelength, it makes a low sound. If a sound wave has a short wavelength, it has a high sound.

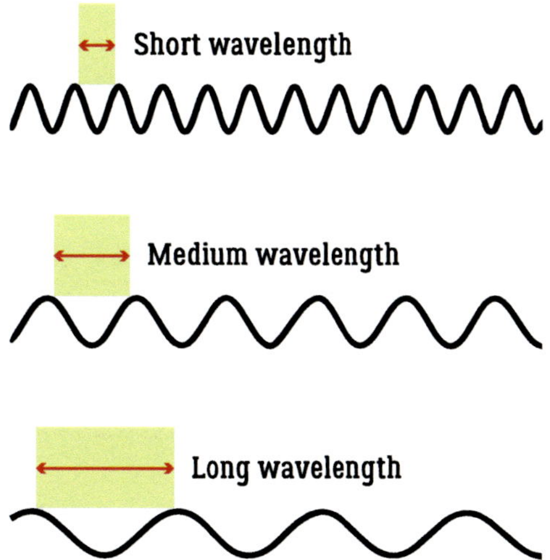

When an object vibrates quickly, it makes a high sound, such as a squeak. When it vibrates slowly, it makes a low sound, like a hum or rumble. The number of vibrations per second is called frequency. Quick vibrations have a high frequency, and slow vibrations have a low frequency.

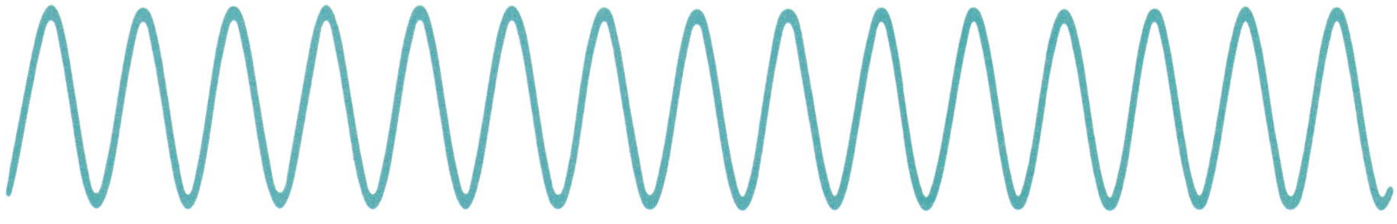

A high-frequency vibration has many waves per second.

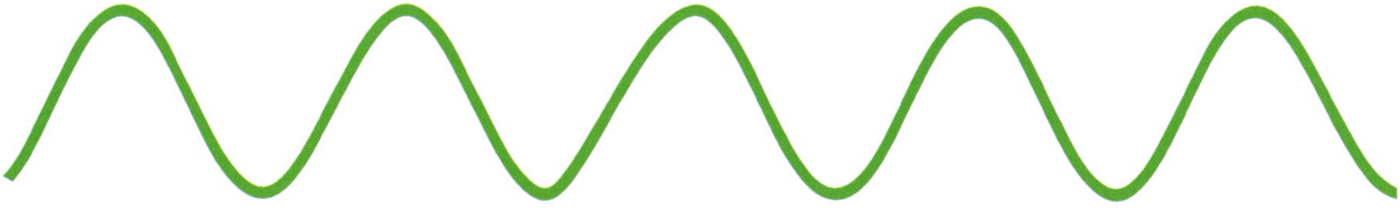

A low-frequency vibration has few waves per second.

THINK LIKE A SCIENTIST!

The best way to learn about science is to do experiments. Scientists use the scientific method to guide what they do. This is a series of questions that help them work in a logical way.

1. Ask a question—this might be based on something you've seen (observed) or on something you've read.

2. Come up with a hypothesis. This is your best guess or prediction for what might happen.

3. Test your hypothesis with an experiment.

4. Write down the results. Did they show what you thought they would?

5. Share the results with other people and ask them to repeat your experiment.

Speed of sound

Sound can travel through anything that can vibrate. It can travel through gases, such as air. It can travel through liquids and solids. Sound moves at different speeds through different materials. It usually travels much faster in solids and liquids than in air.

The speed of sound is the time it takes sound to travel through the air. This is usually about 761 miles per hour (1,225 km/h). But sound doesn't always travel through air at the same speed. It moves faster through dry air than wet air, and it is faster in warm air than cold air.

GET READY

All of the experiments in this book are about sound and hearing. You can do them in any order. Before you start, check that you have all the items you need. Most of the supplies can be found at home, but you might have to get some from a store. Make sure that you have enough space to carry out the experiment. Check with an adult before you start—some of the experiments might get a bit messy! Also ask an adult for help with anything that uses sharp tools or flames. Most of all, have fun!

BOUNCING WAVES

In this experiment, you'll make a sound detector. Can sound make an object move? Use your detector to find out!

WHAT YOU NEED:
- white cardboard
- pen and pencil
- ruler
- balloon
- large can, open at both ends
- rubber band
- small mirror
- flashlight
- Scotch tape

1. Use the ruler and pen to draw lines up and down the cardboard to make a grid of squares. Each square should measure 2 × 2 inches (5 × 5 cm).

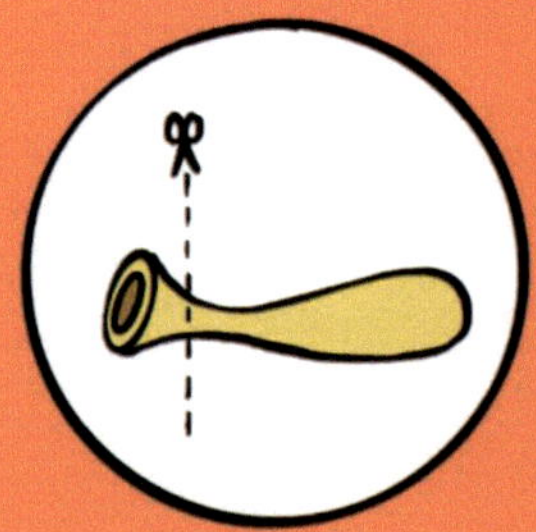

2. Cut the end off the balloon to make a large sheet of rubber.

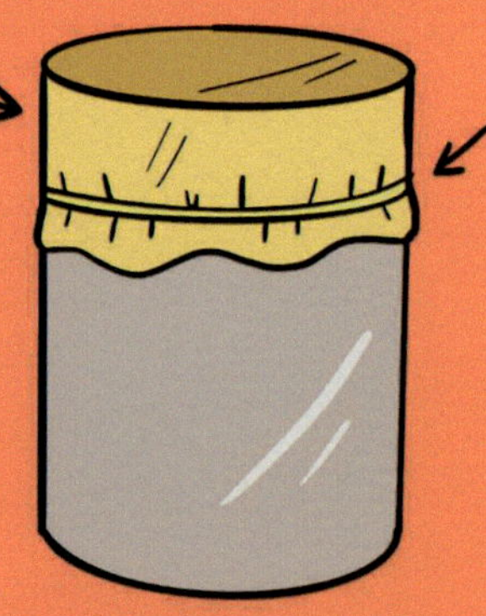

3. Ask an adult to tape around the ends of the can to cover any sharp edges. Stretch the balloon over one end of the can. Hold it in place with a rubber band.

STEM CONCEPTS:
sound waves, vibration

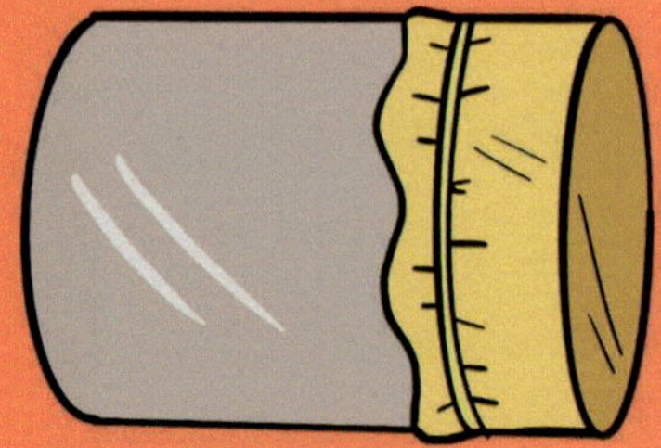

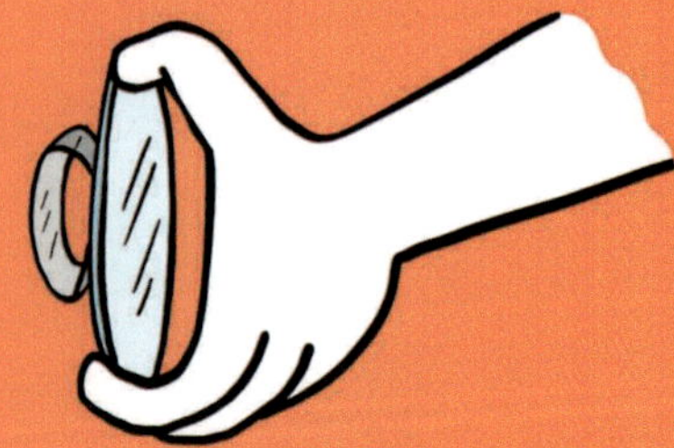

4. Tape the mirror to the balloon.

5. Prop your cardboard grid against a pile of books so that it stands upright. Put the can and flashlight on the table so that the light from the flashlight shines on the mirror and reflects onto the grid.

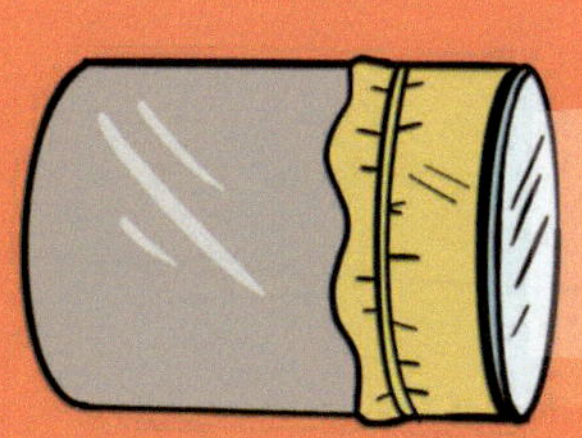

6. Make a mark in the square where the light is shining.

7. Clap your hands together, about 2 feet (60 cm) behind the can. The light should move from one part of the grid to another. Make a mark in that square.

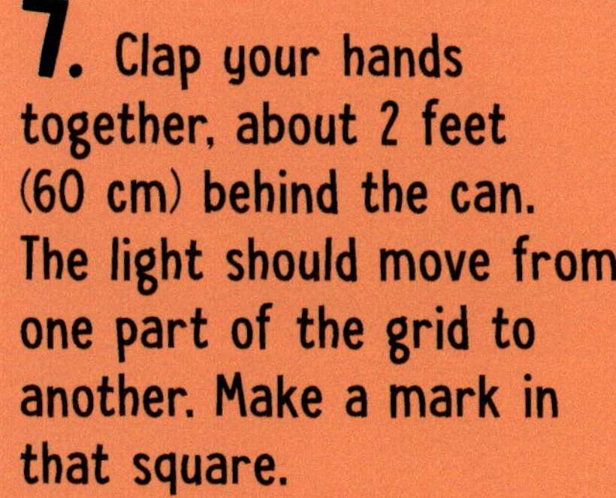

THE SCIENCE BEHIND IT...

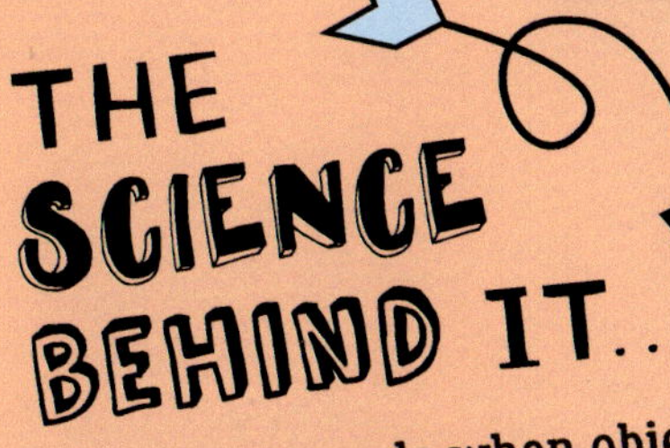

Sounds are made when objects vibrate, but sounds can make objects vibrate. When you clap your hands, sound waves travel to the balloon, hit it, and make it move a little. The mirror also moves, and the flashlight shows by how much.

8. Clap your hands 6 inches (15 cm) behind the can. Make another mark in the square where the light moves to. Measure the distances between the original mark and the two marks you made when you clapped your hands. How far did the light jump this time?

SPOT THE NOISE

Why do we have two ears? One reason is that it helps us spot where a sound is coming from. Test this by building a simple sound locator.

WHAT YOU NEED:

- 4 plastic funnels
- scissors
- tape
- ruler or piece of wooden dowel about 3 feet (1 m) long
- modeling clay
- stool or chair
- blindfold
- alarm clock, radio, or other source of sound
- a friend
- 2 pieces of flexible plastic tubing, about 4 feet (1.2 m) long

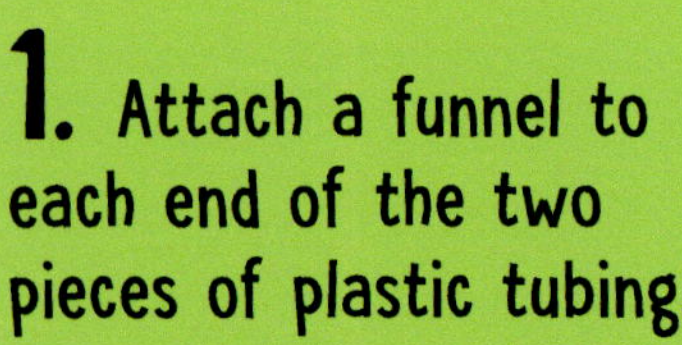

1. Attach a funnel to each end of the two pieces of plastic tubing.

2. Tape one funnel to each end of the ruler.

3. Put a piece of modeling clay onto the stool. Push the ruler into the clay to hold it in place.

STEM CONCEPTS:
hearing, sound location

4. Cover your eyes with the blindfold and hold the two free funnels to your ears. Ask a friend to make a noise using the clock or radio or whatever you are using.

THE SCIENCE BEHIND IT...

Our ears take in sound and send it to the brain. If the sound source is to your right, the sound waves reach your right ear first. The sound will sound louder in your right ear than in the left. Your brain puts this information together to work out where the sound is coming from. Try listening for the sound source with one ear covered up. It should be harder to figure out the position of the sound source.

5. Ask your friend to stand somewhere in the room and set off the sound source. Keep the blindfold on. Point toward the place where you think the sound is coming from.

6. Repeat this a few times. Ask your friend to keep a note of where they were standing, and if you were right about the location of the sound.

SPEED OF SOUND

You've probably heard people talk about the speed of sound. But did you know that you can measure it? Follow these steps to find out how.

WHAT YOU NEED:

- measuring tape
- a wall outside with lots of empty space around it
- chalk
- lid of a trash can
- spoon
- stopwatch

1. Use the measuring tape to measure a distance of 150 feet (45.7 m) from the wall. Mark it with chalk. Carefully measure the same distance again and make another chalk mark. If the two marks are not in exactly the same place, draw a line halfway between them. This will make your distance measurement more accurate.

THE SCIENCE BEHIND IT...

In this activity you measured the time it took for sound waves to travel to the wall and back 20 times. Measuring the sound 20 times makes the experiment more accurate. It gives you more time to stop the clock accurately. The speed of sound is about 1,125 feet (343 m) per second. Was your answer close?

STEM CONCEPTS: sound waves, speed, echoes

2. Stand next to your friend on the chalk mark, facing the wall. One person makes a loud noise by banging on the lid of the trash can. The other person should start the stopwatch as the trash can lid is hit.

3. As soon as you hear the echo, hit the lid of the trash can again. Repeat this 20 times. Stop the watch after the you hear the twentieth echo. Write down the total time taken for the experiment.

To work out the speed of sound, divide the total distance traveled by the sound by the time on the stopwatch. Your answer will be give the speed of sound in feet per second.

TUNING FORK

Try this experiment to find the wavelength of sounds made inside a hollow tube. Find out how the wavelength changes with pitch.

WHAT YOU NEED:

- bucket about two-thirds full of water
- long plastic or card stock tube open at both ends
- tuning forks of several different pitches
- ruler and pen

2. Keep the fork held just above the tube. Listen as you lift the tube out of the water. Keep listening until you find a point where the sound is loudest.

1. Hold the tube in the bucket of water with the top of the tube sticking out of the water. Strike one of the tuning forks on a table. Hold it over the open end of the tube.

3. Mark where the water level is on the side of the tube.

4. Take the tube out of the water. Measure the distance from the mark to the top of the tube (the end that has not been in the water). Write down the result in your notebook.

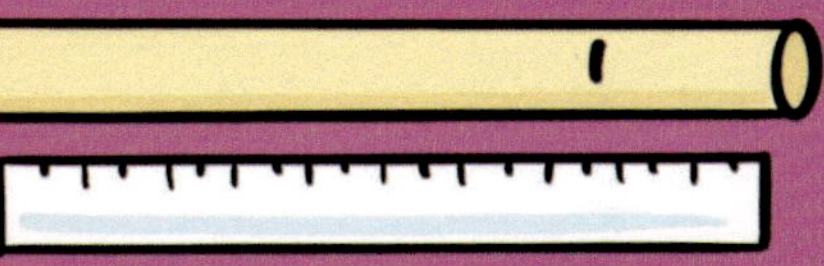

5. Put the tube back in the water. Keep moving it up and down until you find a second spot where the sound is loudest. Mark it with a pen.

THE SCIENCE BEHIND IT...

When you lift the tube from the water, more of the tube can resonate. That makes the air inside the tube vibrate at a lower frequency until it matches the fork's frequency. At this point, the sounds waves inside the tube are loudest because a standing wave has formed. Sound waves repeat themselves. In a long tube, standing waves form in several places. The second loud point is made by another standing wave.

6. Measure the distance from the second mark to the end of the tube. Record this distance. Now take a tuning fork of a different pitch. Repeat steps 1 to 4. Each time, write down your results in your notebook.

BALLOON SOUND

Can you make sound travel more slowly? Try this experiment to find out!

WHAT YOU NEED:
- plastic bottle with a narrow neck
- funnel
- 2 tablespoons of baking powder
- 2 tablespoons of vinegar
- balloon
- string
- Scotch tape
- saucer
- radio

1. Pour the baking powder into the plastic bottle through the funnel. Add the vinegar. The baking powder and vinegar take part in a chemical reaction, which makes carbon dioxide gas.

2. Quickly stretch a balloon over the neck of the bottle. The balloon will inflate as it fills with carbon dioxide gas. When the balloon is fully inflated, tie some string around the neck.

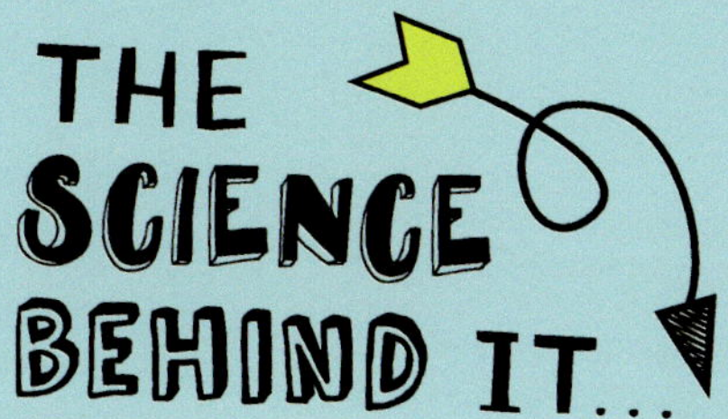

Sound travels at different speeds through different materials. Carbon dioxide is denser than air. The sound waves took longer to travel through the carbon dioxide in the balloon than through the air outside the balloon. That concentrated the sound inside the balloon, which made the radio sound louder though the balloon.

3. Tape the balloon to the saucer so that it does not move.

4. Put the radio about 1.5 feet (45 cm) from the balloon. Switch the radio on and turn up the volume. Put your ear to the other side of the balloon. Move your head until you find the point where the sound is loudest. Turn down the radio until you can only just hear it. (If you cannot reach, ask a friend to turn it down while you listen.)

5. Now take away the balloon. Does the radio sound louder or quieter?

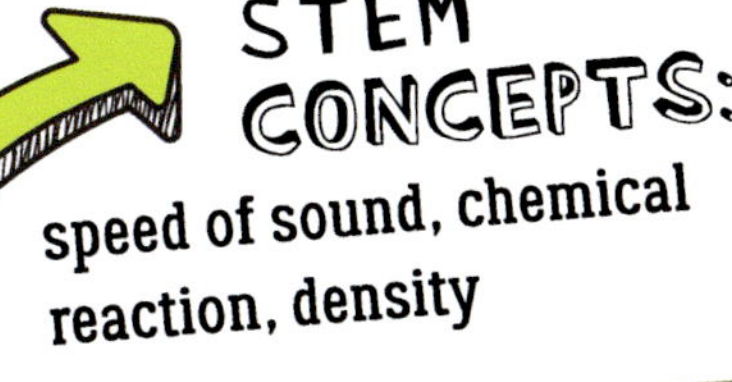

speed of sound, chemical reaction, density

PLUCK A STRING

Make a string instrument. Find out how you can change it to make its pitch higher or lower.

WHAT YOU NEED:

- large, empty can
- hook
- modeling clay
- ruler
- piece of elastic
- plastic bottle
- weights, such as metal nuts or coins

1. Ask an adult to push the hook into the bottom of the can, 1–2 inches (2.5–5 cm) to one side.

2. Use modeling clay to stick the ruler to the opposite edge of the can so that it stands on one of its long edges.

3. Tie one end of the elastic around the hook and the other end to the plastic bottle. Drop a few weights into the bottle. Hang the bottle over the edge of a table so that the elastic goes over the ruler.

THE SCIENCE BEHIND IT...

Different pitches, or notes, have different frequencies. Adding weight to the bottle increased the tension of the elastic. That made the pitch higher. Tightening the string on a stringed instrument makes a higher frequency and therefore a higher pitch. The pitch is also affected by the length of the string. The longer the string, the lower its frequency and the lower the note.

4. Pluck the elastic with your finger, just behind the ruler. Listen to the note that it makes.

5. Put more weights in the bottle and pluck the elastic again. How does the pitch change? Repeat the experiment several times with different weights.

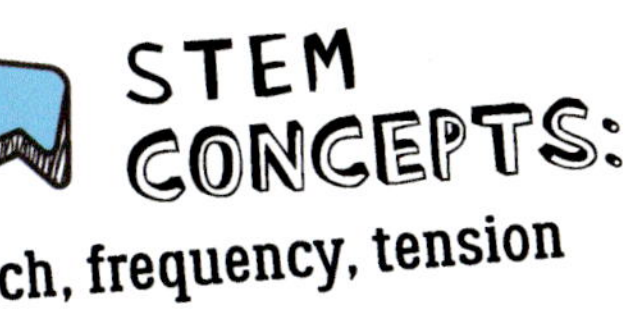

STEM CONCEPTS:

pitch, frequency, tension

PAN PIPES

A piece of music has lots of different notes or pitches. How do musicians change notes as they play? Make some pan pipes and find out.

WHAT YOU NEED:

- drinking straws
- ruler
- pen or pencil
- scissors
- Scotch tape

1. Mark the first straw at 8 inches (20.3 cm) and cut it.

ALWAYS ASK AN ADULT TO HELP WHEN USING SHARP SCISSORS.

2. Repeat with six more straws. Make each straw 1 inch (2.5 cm) shorter than the last.

STEM CONCEPTS:
pitch, frequency, sound waves, wavelength

3. Line the straws up from longest to shortest. Use the ruler to straighten them at the top. Tape them together to make your straw pipe.

THE SCIENCE BEHIND IT...

To make a particular note, a musical instrument has to produce a sound wave of a certain length. When you blow across the tops of the straws, the air inside the straws vibrates. The straws are different lengths and the air in them vibrates with different frequencies. This makes a range of notes. The shortest straw has the highest frequency and should make the highest note.

4. Blow across the top of your pipe. Notice how the pitch changes as the straws get shorter or longer.

MAKE A BEAT

WHAT YOU NEED:
- 2 slide whistles (whistles with a piston that moves in and out)
- 12-inch (30 cm) ruler
- stopwatch
- a notebook and pen
- a friend

Can you make beats with sound? Follow these steps to find out. Hear how the beats change with time.

1. Take one whistle, and give the other one to your friend. Pull the piston of each whistle out halfway. Ask your friend to blow into their whistle and play the same note. Move the piston of your whistle until your note sounds the same as your friend's whistle.

2. Slowly pull out your whistle's piston. You should hear the volume of the sounds made by the two whistles rising and falling in beats. Pull your piston farther out so the two notes are even more different. The changes in volume should get quicker and quicker until you can no longer hear them.

3. Repeat step 1. This time, measure the length of pistons sticking out from your whistles.

Slowly pull the piston out of your whistle until you begin to hear beats. Start the stopwatch when the beats are loudest. Measure the time it takes to make ten beats.

Write down the time it takes to make ten beats as well with the distance that the piston is sticking out of your whistle.

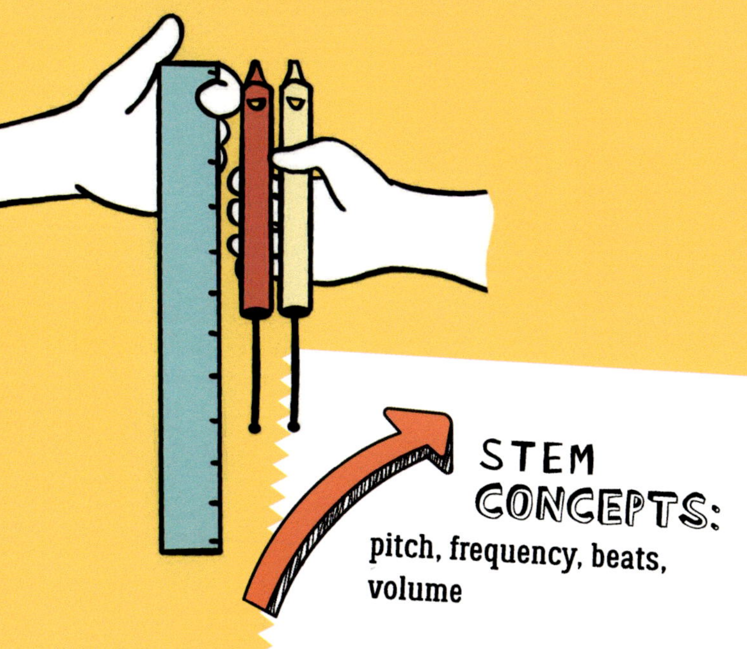

STEM CONCEPTS:
pitch, frequency, beats, volume

4. Pull your piston out a bit more until you hear the beats speed up a little. Write down the time it takes to make ten beats. Measure how far your piston is sticking out of the whistle.

5. Keep repeating step 4 until you can no longer hear any beats.

THE SCIENCE BEHIND IT...

You should have heard no beats when the two pistons were the same length. Making the piston of one whistle longer made its pitch slightly different from the other whistle. The different frequencies mixed and that made the sound beats.

BLOCK THE NOISE

Sometimes we want to block unwanted sound. Try this experiment to learn which materials provide the best sound insulation.

WHAT YOU NEED:

- small radio
- different materials, such as cardboard, padded envelopes, rubber sheeting, and polystyrene
- Scotch tape
- cushion or pillow
- ruler
- scissors

1. Cut out pieces of different materials into a shape that covers the speaker of the radio. The pieces should be a bit bigger than the speaker by about ½ inch (1.25 cm) all the way around.

STEM CONCEPTS:
sound waves, insulation, energy, density, materials

2. Each piece of material should be at least ½ inch (1.25 cm) thick. If the material is too thin, cut out several other pieces. Tape them together until the shape is the right thickness.

3. Turn on the radio and rest it on a cushion. This will absorb any sounds coming from the back. Put one of the materials over the speaker. Slowly turn down the volume until you can't hear the sound. Read the number on the volume knob, and write it in a table next to the name of the material.

THE SCIENCE BEHIND IT...

As a sound wave moves through a material, it loses energy and gets fainter. Some materials are better at absorbing sound than others. They are better sound insulators. In general, dense materials, such as polystyrene, absorb more sound than less dense materials, such as paper. Soft materials, such as cushions, absorb more sound than hard materials, such as cardboard.

4. Repeat step 3 with each material.

BUILD A BULL-ROARER

When a car speeds along a street, its sound changes as it passes you. Investigate this effect with a cardboard tube and some string!

WHAT YOU NEED:

- cardboard tube or strip of thick cardboard made into a tube
- 3-foot (1 m) length of thick string
- blindfolded friend

1. Ask an adult to make two holes at one end of the tube. Thread the string through the holes. Tie it securely.

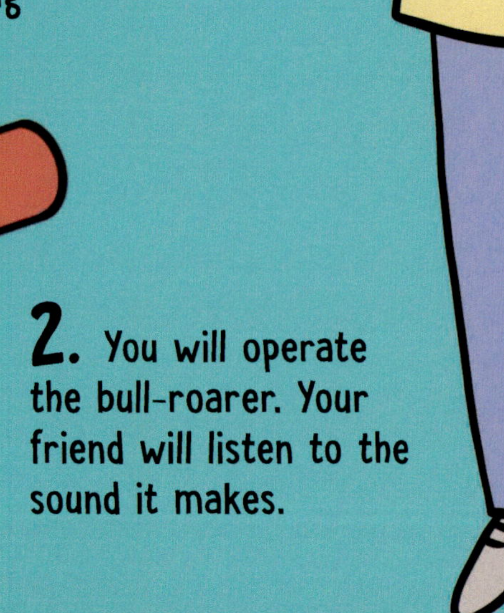

2. You will operate the bull-roarer. Your friend will listen to the sound it makes.

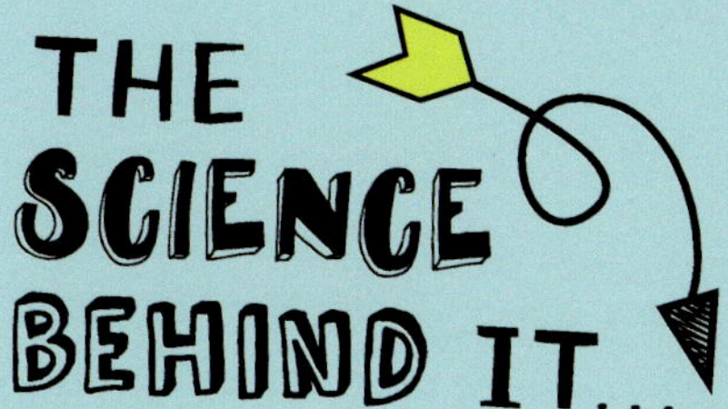

When a sound source changes in relation to where you are standing, its pitch changes. When you were the listener, you should have heard the pitch of the bull-roarer drop as it moved past you. When you were swinging the bull-roarer, the pitch should have stayed the same. The Doppler effect should have been so noticeable that you could tell exactly when the bull-roarer moved past you.

3. Ask your friend to stand about 30 feet (10 m) away from you. Swirl the bull-roarer around your head at a steady speed. Make a sound that has a continuous pitch.

4. Ask your friend to wear a blindfold and listen to the pitch of the note.

30 feet (10 m)

STEM CONCEPTS:
change in pitch, Doppler effect, forces

5. Walk along a straight line in front of your friend while you swing the bull-roarer at a constant speed. Have your friend spot the moment when you walk past them by listening for a shift in the pitch of the bull-roarer. This is called the Doppler effect.

6. Swap roles with your friend and repeat the experiment.

TIPS:

The forces acting on the bull-roarer increase the faster you swing it around. Make sure you tie the string securely to the cardboard tube. It's best to do this experiment outside so you don't damage or break anything. Make sure that you and your friend stand a safe distance apart. Remember, one of you is wearing a blindfold and could wander into the path of the bull-roarer.

A CLAP OF THUNDER

Thunder is the loud noise we hear in a thunderstorm. But what makes it? Follow these steps to find out!

WHAT YOU NEED:

- plastic sheet
- Scotch tape
- rubber gloves
- large iron or steel cooking pot (not aluminum) with a plastic handle
- iron or steel fork
- plastic ruler

1. Tape the plastic sheet onto a tabletop.

2. Put on the rubber gloves.

3. Hold the cooking pot by its handle. Rub it on the plastic sheet.

STEM CONCEPTS:

static electricity, heat, electrical conduction

4. Take the fork in your other hand. Bring it near the cooking pot. A tiny spark of static electricity should jump across the gap between the pot and the fork. You should be able to hear the spark as it jumps. This is like a tiny rumble of thunder.

5. Repeat the activity using a plastic ruler instead of a fork. What happens now?

THE SCIENCE BEHIND IT...

Inside a thundercloud, millions of frozen raindrops rub against each other. This makes electricity. If too much electricity builds up, a giant electric spark jumps to another thundercloud or to the ground. We see this as lightning. When lightning is released, it makes a lot of heat. This makes the air around the cloud expand very quickly, making a loud, rumbling noise—thunder. In this experiment, an electrical spark jumps from the pan to the metal fork because metal conducts electricity. It doesn't jump to the plastic ruler because plastic doesn't conduct electricity.

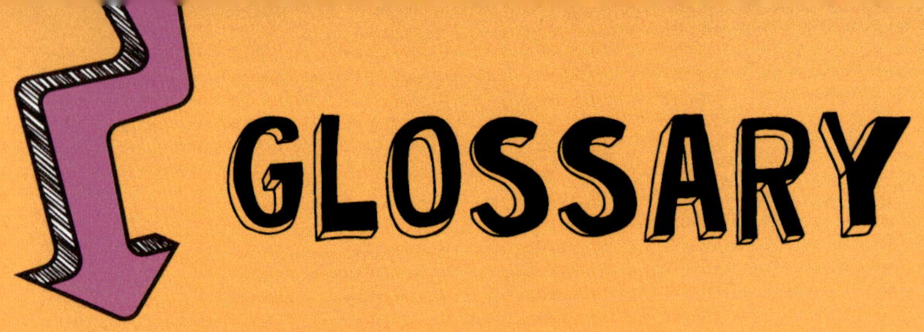

GLOSSARY

Aluminum a type of metal

Beat when two slightly different pitches combine to make a regular, pulsing sound

Carbon dioxide a colorless gas found in the air

Doppler effect the apparent change in the frequency of a sound wave as the source of the sound moves toward or away from someone listening to it

Echo the reflection of a sound wave

Energy a force that moves or changes matter

Frequency the speed at which a sound wave vibrates

Gas one of the states of matter. Gases have no fixed volume or shape.

Insulator a material that slows or blocks the movement of sound, heat, or electricity

Liquid one of the states of matter. Liquids have a fixed volume but no shape. They take on the shape of their container.

Pitch how high or low a sound is, determined by the frequency of the waves producing it

Resonate to vibrate strongly

Solid one of the states of matter. Solids have a fixed volume and a fixed shape.

Sound wave an invisible curved pattern of movement of sound energy through a material

Speed the distance traveled in a set time

Standing wave the pattern of vibrations in a long, thin object

Tension a force that stretches or pulls something

Vibrate to move backward and forward about a fixed point

FURTHER RESOURCES

BOOKS

Chatteron, Crystal. **Awesome Science Activities for Kids.** Rockridge Press, 2018.

Claybourne, Anna. **Can You Hear Sounds in Space? And Other Questions about Sound.** Wayland, 2020.

Glover, David. **Discover It Yourself: Sound and Light.** Kingfisher, 2021.

WEBSITES

www.ducksters.com/science/sound101.php
Visit this website to learn the basics about sound.

easyscienceforkids.com/cool-sound-vibrations-video-for-kids/
This website has some fun facts about sound.

kids.britannica.com/students/article/sound/277144
Find out what sound is, how it is made and carried, and how musical instruments produce sound.

Publisher's note to educators and parents: Our editors have carefully reviewed these websites to ensure that they are suitable for students. Many websites change frequently, however, and we cannot guarantee that a site's future contents will continue to meet our high standards of quality and educational value. Be advised that students should be closely supervised whenever they access the internet.

INDEX

Air 7, 14, 15, 17, 21, 29

Beats 22, 23

Brain 11

Carbon dioxide 16, 17

Doppler effect 27

Ears and hearing 4, 7, 10, 11

Frequency 5, 15, 19, 20, 21, 23

Gases 7

Hypothesis 6

Liquids 7

Metal 18, 29

Musical instruments 4, 18, 19, 20, 21, 22, 23

Particles 4

Pitch 14, 15, 18, 19, 20, 21, 23, 27

Resonance 15

Scientific method 6

Solids 7

Sound detector 8

Sound insulation 24, 25

Sound waves 4, 5, 8, 9, 11, 13, 15, 17, 20, 21, 24, 25

Speed of sound 7, 12, 13, 17

Standing wave 15

Static electricity 29

Vibrations 4, 5, 8

Wavelength 5, 14, 20